Speaking and Listening

# Yackety-yak, the Alien's Back

Pie Corbett
and Ruth Thomson

Chrysalis Education

Distributed in the United States by
Smart Apple Media
2140 Howard Drive West
North Mankato, Minnesota 56003

Copyright © Chrysalis Books Group PLC 2004

Library of Congress Control Number 2004100724

ISBN 1-59389-141-5

**Editorial manager**: Joyce Bentley
**Editor**: Nicola Edwards
**Designers**: Rachel Hamdi, Holly Mann
**Illustrators**: Jan McCafferty, Guy Parker-Rees,
Liz Pichon, and Gwyneth Williamson

Printed in China

# Contents

# Speaking and listening

Talking helps children to think, communicate, and make sense of the world around them. Children's speech flourishes where there are interesting activities to discuss. This happens through play, describing what is happening around them, looking at interesting objects and books, and talking about events at home or in school.

Recounting what the family or class has done and inventing stories together

Yackety-yak, I'm big and I'm back!

are helpful ways to develop talk and the imagination. Saying funny sentences, inventing rhymes, and singing are also important.

## About this book

This book is designed for adults (whether parents, carers, or teachers) and children to talk about together. It is brimming with activities that will give children opportunities to talk out loud, develop their abilities to speak in a wide variety of ways, and listen carefully.

### The activities

Each double page has a particular focus (see the contents page) and is completely self-contained. You can open the book at any page, talk together about what you see in the detailed pictures, and go backward or forward at whim.

Although the book has no fixed order, the activities in the first half are generally easier than those in the second half. The early pages encourage children to play with words, use alliteration, create riddles, and describe and compare, using complex sentences. Later pages stimulate children to respond at greater length, complaining, advising, making up stories, and problem solving.

You do not need to do all the activities on each page at one sitting. The book has been deliberately

designed to be re-read again and again, with more things to discover at each re-reading.

### Extension activities

There are further suggestions of things to do related to each theme on pages 30 and 31. These, in turn, may prompt you to invent more activities of your own.

### Talking and listening guidelines

There are suggested guidelines for how good speakers and listeners behave on page 32.

# How to use this book

The four activities at the bottom of each double page provide starting points for conversation. Some invite children to discuss what they see and to use talk in an exploratory way. Others require a more formal response, using particular sentence structures and vocabulary. In some cases, sentence openers or models are given. These are merely suggestions for developing different types of sentence or vocabulary, such as comparatives or the use of time connectives (e.g. then, after), which will help children develop their talk beyond one or two-word comments. You could also move from a talking session into writing.

The pictures have been drawn so that there are usually many different possible responses, as an atmosphere of "getting it right or wrong" will not encourage children to speak up. Children talk best when they feel relaxed and the people around them are interested in what they have to say. If children seem uncertain, begin by modeling a sentence structure (the text preceded by the speech bubble). Try to avoid asking questions that require one word answers. Use phrases such as "tell me…," which invite more extended replies.

## Talk partners

You may find it helpful to ask the children to "think, share in a pair," before giving a response in front of a whole class. Working with a talk partner provides a chance to think together and plan what might be said. It is also helpful if you can model a few possible responses, so that the children might listen and think carefully for themselves before they rehearse their own reply in pairs and say it aloud in front of the class.

The focus of the talking activity.

The talking activity that you ask the child to do.

A sample answer you might expect from the child.

The sentence structure you could encourage the child to use.

**What's all the fuss?**
Describe what you can see.

★ **What can you see?**
List three things that you can see on the pirate ship, using only one sentence.
◯ **On the pirate ship I can see** a boy mopping the deck, a cook carrying a fish **and** a dog fast asleep.

★ **Watch out!**
Choose a pirate in the first picture and warn him or her about what is about to happen.
◯ **Watch out because** the hammock is about to collapse!

★ **How are they feeling?**
Choose someone in the second picture. Explain how they are feeling, and why.
◯ The pirate in the crow's nest is cross **because** a seagull has flown off with her hat.

★ **What next?**
Choose something that is happening in the second picture and say what might happen next.
◯ The sharks might eat the pirate who has been pulled overboard.

14

15

# A wonderful world of wildlife
## Use sounds and rhymes.

★ **I see**

Play "I see" using sounds or letters, e.g. **"t."**
Try using beginning, end, or middle sounds.

◯ **I see** two things **that end with "t."**

◯ Goa**t** and new**t** both end with "t."

★ **Rhyme it**

In the picture, find things that rhyme with **bar**, **toy**, **how**, **stair,** and **poor**. Then choose a creature, e.g. **fox**, and think of a word that rhymes with it.

◯ Box **rhymes with** fox.

## ✦ Alphabet challenge

Look for animals for each letter of the alphabet. How many creatures can you find that start with the same letter?

🗨 **K**angaroo and **k**oala both start with "k."

## ✦ Riddles

Choose an animal, e.g. an owl, and make up three clues about it. Who can guess your riddle?

🗨 **I am thinking of an animal that** starts with "o," rhymes with "trowel," and flies at night.

# What is it like?

Play with words.

★ **Invent riddles**

Choose an object, e.g. the spade, and make up three clues about it. Who can guess your riddle?

○ I am made of wood and metal. I work by digging deep. Birds sit on me when I rest.

★ **Crazy sentences**

Choose an object. Pretend that it comes alive. Make up a crazy sentence about it.

○ The sack sat in the corner twiddling its thumbs.

**★ Invent tongue twisters**

Choose an object and invent a tongue twister about it.

◯ The **s**ilver, **s**lippery **s**aw **s**ailed **s**ilently as the **s**lithery **s**nake **s**neaked by **s**lyly.

**★ Create similes**

Choose an object and invent a simile about it.

◯ **The broom is like** a giraffe's neck.

**The broom is like** a bushy mustache.

**The moon is like** a slice of lemon!

# Alien spotting
## Find similarities and differences.

★ **Which one?**

Take it in turns to describe an alien
for someone else to find.

○ This alien has…

★ **Spot the similarities**

Choose two aliens that share two similarities
for someone else to find.

○ These two aliens both have…

★ **Spot the difference**

Choose two or three aliens.

Explain how they are different.

💬 These aliens are different **because** one has...
and the other one has...

★ **Similarities and differences**

Point to two aliens. Explain how they are
similar and how they are different.

💬 These aliens **both have**... **and**...**but**...

# Who lives where?
## Use descriptive language.

✦ **Matching game**

Describe a character and the house they live in. Who can match the character to the house?

💬 Which lady in red with the flowery hat lives at the house with the green door?

✦ **Tell me where**

Choose a house or character and give three clues about where it is. Use words like "below, above, beside, behind, near, next to, and in-between." Who can guess the house or character you have chosen?

💬 Which house is **between**...?

✦ **Ask questions**

Take turns to ask a question about a person or house for someone else to answer.

💬 Which is the house with a cat on the roof?

✦ **Spot the difference**

Choose a pair of houses or characters and explain the differences between them.

💬 **The differences between... and... are that...**

# What's all the fuss?
## Describe what you can see.

★ **What can you see?**

List three things that you can see on the pirate ship, using only one sentence.

💬 **On the pirate ship I can see** a boy mopping the deck, a cook carrying a fish, **and** a dog fast asleep.

★ **Watch out!**

Choose a pirate in the first picture and warn him or her about what is about to happen.

💬 **Watch out, because** the hammock is about to collapse!

★ **How are they feeling?**

Choose someone in the second picture.
Explain how they are feeling, and why.

◯ The pirate in the crow's nest is cross
**because** a sea gull has flown off with her hat.

★ **What next?**

Choose something that is happening in the second
picture and say what might happen next.

◯ The sharks might eat the pirate who has been
pulled overboard.

# Find the way
## Give directions.

**✦ Find the stall**

Choose a stall and give three clues about where it is. Use words like "below, above, beside, behind, near, next to, and in-between." Who can guess the stall you have chosen?

💬 Which stall **has a**...and is in **front of**...and **next to**...?

**✦ Which way?**

Choose two stalls and describe how you would get from one stall to the other.

💬 **To get from** the stall selling fish **to** the stall selling eggs **I would**...

**✦ This way!**

Choose a character and give them instructions about how to get to a stall. Use words like "turn left, turn right, go along, keep going straight-ahead."

💬 Mrs. Singh, **to get to the** book stall...

**✦ Time for hot drinks**

Give each character instructions for how to get to the hot-drinks stall.

💬 Mr. Williams, **to get to the hot-drinks stall**...

Mike Smith

Jackie Lee

Mr. Williams

Paula Cortez

Mrs. Young

Dr. Chang

Singh

Bill Stone

# Whatever next? Tell the tale.

★ **What's happening?**

Choose a set of pictures and tell the story of what is happening.

◯ The princess was locked in the tower. A prince came to rescue her, but he hadn't noticed the dragon...

★ **What happened before?**

Invent a sentence to explain what has happened before the set of pictures, starting with the word "before."

◯ **Before** she was captured by the dragon, the princess...

★ **Talk to them**

Imagine you could talk to the different characters. What would you say to each other?

💬 Watch out! There's a dragon behind you!

💬 Thanks! What's it doing?

★ **What happens next?**

Invent a sentence to explain what happens next, using the word "after."

💬 **After** the prince saw the dragon, there was a fierce fight.

# Work it out!
## Complain and give advice.

★ **What's up?**

Choose a problem and explain what has gone wrong.

◯ The hot-air balloon has a puncture and all the gas is coming out. The passengers in the basket are looking worried.

★ **Complain**

Work in pairs. Imagine one of you has taken the faulty goods back. Complain to the salesperson.

◯ This hot-air balloon has got a puncture. You should give me a new one!

★ **Silly solutions**

Suggest silly ways to solve the problem.

💬 **Can I suggest that you** use some chewing gum to mend the puncture and then the balloon will fly beautifully.

★ **What next?**

Choose something that is going wrong in the picture. Tell the story of what happens next.

💬 The balloon began to fall to the ground. Luckily, it landed on soft sand and everyone was saved.

# Danger island
## Describe the dangers and give advice.

★ **What will happen?**

There is trouble ahead on Danger Island!
Take it in turns to suggest what might happen.

💬 If the man steps on the snake, **then** the snake might bite him!

★ **What would they say?**

Say what you think each person might shout out.

💬 Help! the tree is shaking!
Oh no! That bear looks hungry!

★ **Impossible advice**

Tell the people how to avoid disaster. Invent impossible ideas for how they could escape.

⌕ **To avoid** being eaten by the crocodile, simply grow wings and fly away.

★ **You'll never guess...**

Pretend you are one of the people on the island and tell a friend what happened to you.

⌕ It was so hot that I wanted to cool off. So, I jumped into the water. Suddenly, a shark appeared...

# The story café
## Pick ingredients for a story.

★ **Choose a goodie**

Pick a "goodie" as your main character. (Choose from those at the table below.) Think about where your character might live. Invent three things about your character.

🗩 **There was once** a cat called Frankie, who lived in a forest. She had sleek, ginger fur and she loved eating mangoes.

★ **Choose a magical object**

Pick a magical object for your character to find. What magical powers does the object have?

🗩 The magic cloak makes anyone who puts it on able to fly.

★ **Pick a baddie**

Choose a "baddie" from the opposite page for your story. What is he or she like? Where does he or she live? Invent three things about your character.

🗩 The snake lives in a cave. It can destroy things by breathing on them. It never tells the truth.

★ **Making links**

Practice making links between your goodie, your baddie, and the magical object. Use the story connectives on the menu board in the story café.

🗩 **Suddenly**, the snake appeared. **As** it slithered towards her, Frankie wrapped herself in the magic cloak.

• Now turn the page and use your characters to tell a story about a journey.

# The story island
## Mix ingredients for a story.

✦ **Pick a setting**

Choose a place on the island where your character will begin his or her journey. What is the place like? Why is your character there?

💬 Frankie lived in the forest, underneath her favorite mango tree. The forest was dark and silent.

✦ **Choose a destination**

Pick a place where your character's journey will end. Why is the journey necessary?

💬 Frankie has to travel to the cave in the mountains to find some medicine for the old king who is ill.

✦ **What happens?**

What goes wrong on the journey? What part does the magical object play? Use the map to think of some ideas. Which baddies does your character meet on the way?

💬 Frankie finds a crystal ball that shows her how to escape from traps. Then she meets a cat-eating troll.

✦ **The end**

How does your character get round all the problems? Tell the story, using connectives and adverbs. How does your story end?

**Story adverbs**

angrily
bravely
carefully
cautiously
desperately
foolishly
quickly
quietly
silently
slowly

# Can you fix it? Solve the problems.

★ **Watch out!**

Find a problem in the picture.

💬 The cat is trying to reach the baby birds.
It might attack them.

★ **Solve it**

Discuss different ideas for solving the problem.

💬 You could... You might... If you...
How about... Supposing...

★ **Will it work?**

Listen to some ideas and discuss their
strengths and weaknesses.

🗨 I like the idea... **because**... **but** you
might find that...

★ **Crazy ideas**

Try inventing some really crazy solutions.

🗨 The cat could put on a snorkel and swim
across to rescue the toy from the pond!

# Extension activities

The pictures in this book are designed to generate talk for all kinds of purposes. When children are talking, encourage them to speak up sufficiently loudly and clearly so that everyone can hear and you do not have to repeat what they have said. Mirror standard versions back to them or ask them to complete what has been said, especially if it is fragmentary or over relies on gesture.

Give praise to those who have listened well and responded with questions or answers. In group or paired work, taking turns is a crucial step forward which needs to be modeled by the teacher and praised. At this age, group work needs careful structuring so that everyone knows their role in the group. This will need practice and discussion.

When a presentation is being given, encourage children to identify key points in what is being said. Focus their listening by asking them to locate specific points and recall them afterward.

Constant inventing, telling and re-telling of stories using traditional language will help children to internalize basic patterns of narrative, including sentence patterns.

Use simple role-play and improvisation to act out scenes based on children's own experiences. These can arise easily out of the pictures in this book by asking children to select characters or an event and have them act it out or discuss what happened.

## Pages 6-7  A wonderful world of wildlife

*This spread provides practice in the ability to identify sounds in words and rhyming patterns. It encourages children to think about letters of the alphabet and create simple riddles. You could also use the spread to focus on sounds in different ways.*

★ Practice simple segmentation by asking children to find animals that have 3 (rat), 4 (tiger), or 5 (koala) sounds.

★ Choose a creature and see who can list the largest number of rhymes, e.g. rat – sat, bat, cat, mat, flat, and so on.

★ Ask the children to role-play the discussion going on in the car!

## Pages 8-9  What is it like?

*These two pages provide practice in inventing simple riddles, simple personification, alliteration, and similes. It is not important for children to know the names of the effects that they are using and the key to the spread is that it should be playful and enjoyable. Give children time to work in pairs inventing their sentences so that they have time to "think" and discuss with their partner before they come together to "share" their ideas.*

★ Ask questions based on the five senses, such as: "Can you find something that is heavy and good to look at?" (e.g. large book).

★ Use the spread to play *I-see*, finding rhymes for different items.

★ Ask the children to describe items and see who can guess what they are describing.

## Pages 10-11  Alien spotting

*This spread is packed with aliens! It can be used to practice simple description and discrimination, thinking about similarities and differences.*

★ Ask the children to name different aliens and consider what they might be able to do. Talk about where they could hide in a house and discuss whether they have superpowers.

★ Ask the children to imagine what might happen if an alien visited their classroom.

★ The children could create their own aliens and add them to the discussion.

## Pages 12-13  Who lives where?

*This spread provides further practice in using precise descriptive language, using positional language such as "above," "beside," or "below" as well as asking questions and spotting differences.*

★ Ask the children to give names to the characters and describe them, e.g. what they are wearing, how they behave, and how they speak. Discuss what they might be like, considering which characters might be goodies and which could be baddies in a story. Discuss what sort of story the characters might be in.

★ Choose a character and act out a simple situation, such as buying a chocolate bar.

★ Use the picture as a starting point for making up stories. Choose only a few of the characters each time and invent conversations among them.

## Pages 14-15  What's all the fuss?

*This spread provides opportunities to use language in different ways, e.g. to describe, to warn and to recount in the past and future tense.*

★ Choose a pirate and discuss what he or she might say in each picture.

★ Put different pirates "in the hot-seat" and ask the children to interview them about what has happened.

★ Invent a television news bulletin about the pirate ship disaster.

★ Work in pairs and hold a discussion about what has happened.

## Pages 16-17  Find the way

*These pages focus on using instructional language to give directions.*

★ Use the spread to develop the children's descriptive skills, e.g. ask them to describe characters or stalls.

★ Ask the children to choose a character and in role pretend to approach a stall and buy something or return an item and complain about its quality.

★ Ask children to pretend they are stallholders trying to persuade customers to buy items. Encourage them to use positive language to persuade their customers to buy the products.

## Pages 18-19  Whatever next?

*The groups of pictures provide opportunities for children to recount what has happened, is happening, and what might happen next.*

✦ Use the pictures as a basis for storytelling. Provide story connectives that could be used, e.g. Once upon a time, one day, early one morning, so, next, when, while, after that, suddenly, without warning, at that moment, finally, in the end, eventually…

✦ To encourage a simple pattern, ask the children to include:
- an opening
- a build-up, in which the story begins
- a dilemma, where something goes wrong
- a resolution, which sorts out the problem
- an ending

✦ Continue the story boards by adding more pictures before and after the three pictures shown. Use these as a simple way to aid plotting.

## Pages 20-21  Work it out!

*This double page sets up a host of different events which lend themselves to complaining and advising, as well as imagining what might happen next. The idea of consequences lies at the root of storytelling.*

✦ Work on simple monologues that have a chosen character talking aloud, describing the various incidents.

✦ Encourage the children to focus on each incident, explaining what is happening and suggesting how it might be resolved.

✦ The children could pretend to be journalists and interview characters to discover what happened.

## Pages 22-23  Danger Island

*This double spread encourages children to describe events, using simple recounts. It is built around a series of possible dangers that need to be avoided. It could lend itself to all sorts of possibilities for talk:*

✦ Ask the children to pretend to be a character telling a friend what happened.

✦ Pretending to be television news reporters, children could interview characters about events on the island.

✦ Use the picture as a basis for simple story making.

✦ Ask the children to re-tell events in a diary format.

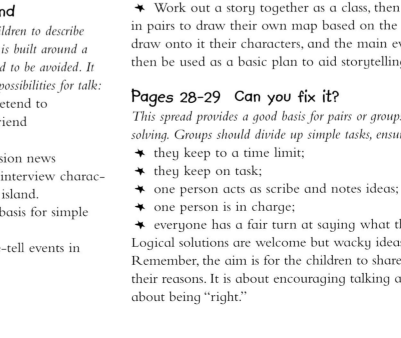

## Pages 24-25  The story café

The pictures on this double page can be used as an imaginative way into story making. The café provides basic ingredients to select from: various characters (goodies and baddies) settings, and magical objects.

✦ Let the children select one goodie who will meet one baddie. Ask them to describe the characters and role-play with them in different situations, e.g. sitting on a bus together. Encourage the children to say descriptive sentences that use detail to make the characters sound real. Try sentences with three elements, e.g. the dragon had green scales, red eyes, and fire belching from its mouth.

✦ Ask the children to think about where the story will start and where the action will take place, encouraging them to invent descriptions for different settings.

✦ What magic object might be involved? Ask the children to describe it and decide on its special powers.

✦ Use question words to begin to flesh out a story idea:
- who are the characters?
- where are they?
- what goes wrong? (the dilemma)
- when is the story set? (past or present tense)
- how will it end?

✦ With the children, scan books to add to the collection of story connectives. Practice sentences using these. If children struggle, invent some together, initially modeling several examples.

## Pages 26-27 The story island

*The picture map provides a chance for children to use it to invent their own story, with a simple structure.*

✦ Who is the main character? Where are they going? Why are they going? (Provide a simple task.) What route will they take? What awful event will befall them en route? (Bring the baddie into play!) Where do they find the magic object and how will it help them escape the main dilemma?

✦ Think about a safe ending.

✦ It is important to use the story connectives to help link the tale together.

✦ Work out a story together as a class, then let children work in pairs to draw their own map based on the spread. They can draw onto it their characters, and the main events. This can then be used as a basic plan to aid storytelling.

## Pages 28-29  Can you fix it?

*This spread provides a good basis for pairs or groups to practice problem-solving. Groups should divide up simple tasks, ensuring that:*

✦ they keep to a time limit;

✦ they keep on task;

✦ one person acts as scribe and notes ideas;

✦ one person is in charge;

✦ everyone has a fair turn at saying what they think.

Logical solutions are welcome but wacky ideas are also fun. Remember, the aim is for the children to share ideas and explain their reasons. It is about encouraging talking and listening, not about being "right."

# How to be a good speaker and listener

When I **speak**, I need to:

* Be ready to ask people to explain ideas further.

* Respect ideas that I don't agree with.

* Add more points to a discussion.

* Give reasons for my ideas: I think. . . because. . .

* Try to keep to the point.

* Use expression to make what I say sound interesting.

* Remember who I am talking with and how they might feel.

* Suggest ideas: What if. . .?

* Be ready to change my mind if I hear a good idea.

* Think of things that might be interesting or useful to say or add.

* Organize what I'm going to say with an introduction, the content, and a conclusion.

* Include relevant details.

* Speak clearly, look at my audience, and take turns.

When I **listen**, I need to:

* Remember instructions and specific points.

* Show by my expression that I am interested in the speaker.

* Write down information or ideas that I might forget.

* Wait my turn before speaking.

* Look at the speaker, keep still, and follow what is being said.

* Ask about anything I don't understand.

* Give a reply if someone asks a question.